First edition for North America published 2013
by Barron's Educational Series, Inc.

Original edition published in 2013
by Hodder Children's Books

Text copyright © Mij Kelly 2013
Illustrations copyright © Charles Fuge 2013

This book was designed and produced by
Hodder Children's Books
338 Euston Road
London, NW1 3BH

All inquiries should be addressed to:
Barron's Educational Series, Inc.
250 Wireless Boulevard
Hauppauge, NY 11788
www.barronseduc.com

ISBN: 978-1-4380-0345-0

Library of Congress Control Number: 2001012345

Date of Manufacture: July 2013
Manufactured by:
South China Printing Company, Dongguan, China

Printed in China
9 8 7 6 5 4 3 2 1

Friendly Day

Mij Kelly and Charles Fuge

BARRON'S

When Cat caught Mouse, outside his house,
courageous Mouse cried, "Hey!
Put down that plate and see the date.
It's **Friendly Day** today

`a day for sharing, a day for caring,
when everyone is nice,

when Frog reads Snail a fairy tale
and cats do NOT eat mice."

"Well fancy that," exclaimed the cat,
"I'll *have* to spread the word!"
He quickly strode across the road,
and told Dog what he'd heard.

Dog stared wide-eyed, and then replied,
"That's such a great idea!
You mean to say, today's the day,
the one day in the year

when parakeets bring tigers treats
and Rhino takes the time
to knit new mittens for helpless kittens

and sing a nursery rhyme?"

Cat cried, "Yes! Yes! And sharks play chess with all the little fishes,

and old grey Moose pours orange juice for anyone that wishes,

and even Mole comes out of his hole
to play I Spy with Goat

and Chimpanzee makes herbal tea
for Ostrich's sore throat."

Dog said, "Oh boy, what joy, what joy!"

And "Hip-hip-hip hooray!"

He called, "Hey Bear, are you aware,

today is friendly day

when foxes croon all afternoon
to entertain the geese,

and little birds tweet soothing words
of **hope** and **love** and **peace**."

Bear scratched his head, and then he said,
"It is a lovely thought,

to think that we could ever be,
as kindly as we ought.

To think baboons hand out balloons
to all the butterflies
makes tears of bliss and happiness,
come pouring from my eyes."

"But Dog," said Bear, "Are you aware,
there's really no such thing
as friendly day, or any day
when wasps and bees don't sting?

I must insist, it doesn't exist.
It is a lovely lie."
Poor Dog. Poor Cat. They hated that.
They both began to cry.

Inside his house, the tiny mouse
was glad he'd slipped away.
He'd tricked the cat, but now he sat
and longed for **friendly day**.

Meanwhile, outside, the dog still cried.
The bear gave him a pat.
"Oh, do cheer up, my dearest pup.
I have a plan," said Cat.

We'll talk to Snail and Snake and Whale.
We'll put the world to rights.
We'll make them see how things could be,

if only no-one fights."

Dog thought of how a friendly cow
might **help** a crocodile,

how centipedes might do
good deeds...
He smiled a watery smile.

Then **arm** in **arm**, with old-world charm
— and so much to be done —
the **three friends** strode off down the road,
towards the setting sun.